For Mum

First U.S. edition 2009

Library of Congress Cataloging-in-Publication Data is available.
Library of Congress Catalog Card Number 2008933309

ISBN 978-0-7636-4272-3

2 4 6 8 10 9 7 5 3

Printed in China

This book was typeset in MT Schoolbook.
The illustrations were done in mixed media.

Candlewick Press
99 Dover Street
Somerville, Massachusetts 02144

visit us at www.candlewick.com

Tilly and
her friends
all live
together in
a little yellow
house. . . .

Pretty
Pru

Polly Dunbar

CANDLEWICK PRESS

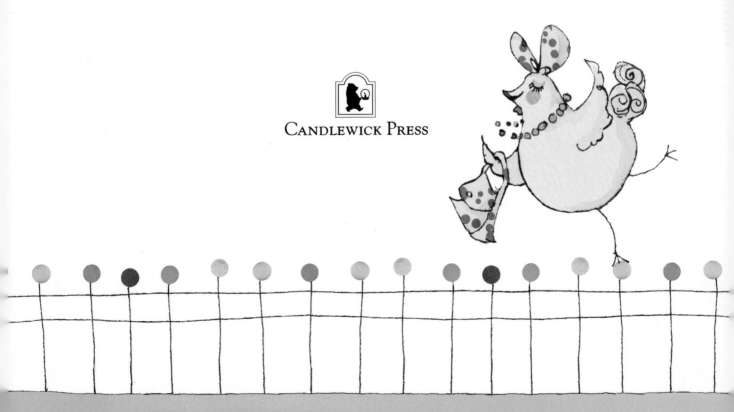

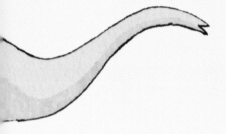

"Oh, pretty,"
said Pru.
"I'm so pretty!"

She was
putting on her
favorite
red lipstick.

"Can I have some makeup?" asked Tumpty.

"Then I can be pretty like you."

"No,"
said Pru.
"You'll
waste it."

"Humpf," said Tumpty.

So while Pru
was busy doing
a pretty-prance . . .

Tumpty stretched out his very
long trunk and took Pru's purse!

"Look, everybody," said Tumpty.

"Now we can be pretty like Pru."

"Tilly, Tilly, Tilly!"
Pru called.
"My purse—
it's lost."

"Don't worry," said Tilly.

"It can't be far away."

"Hello, Hector,"
said Tilly.
"Pru's lost
her purse.
Do you
have it?"

"No," said Hector.

"My purse!"
cried Pru,
"my green
purse
with red
spots.

Tiptoe,
have you seen it?"

Tiptoe blushed

the prettiest shade of pink.

"Doodle!"
said Pru, flapping.
"Have **you**
seen my
purse . . .

with my blush
and nail polish?"

"It wasn't me!" said Doodle,
and she pointed a very pretty finger.

She was
pointing at
Tumpty.

Tumpty was doing
a pretty-prance
of his own.

He looked **extremely funny.**

Everybody laughed—

everybody except Pru.

"That's
my purse
on your head,"
said Pru.

Everybody

stopped laughing.

"I'm sorry,"

Tumpty said.

With a curl of his very long trunk,

he gave Pru back her purse.

"We're sorry, too," said Hector.

And they all put the makeup back in the bag.

Then Pru did
something very special.
She gave Tumpty
her **favorite** red lipstick.

Tumpty did something
very special, too. . . .

He let

everybody

have a turn.

And they all pranced prettily,

just like Pru.

The End